Little Red Riding Hood

Written by
Tony Mitton

Illustrated by
Liz Million

WALKER BOOKS
AND SUBSIDIARIES
LONDON • BOSTON • SYDNEY • AUCKLAND

Big Bad Greedy Wolf has run to Gran's ahead.

Ho-ho!

Little Red Riding Hood says, "Granny, are you there?"

Little Red Riding Hood begins to shout and cry.

In comes the lumberjack to see if he can help.

Ooh!

Out!

Out goes
Big Bad Wolf,
hip, hop, yelp!

Big Bad Greedy Wolf has run off through the wood.

"Time to have some cake," says Gran.
"Doesn't it look good?"

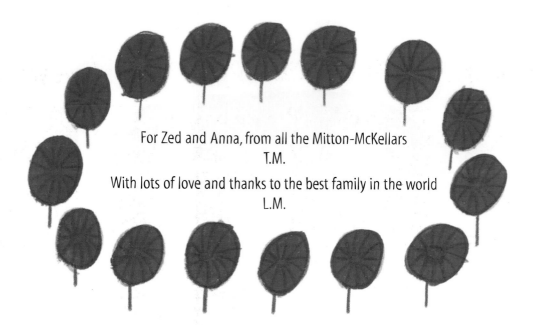

For Zed and Anna, from all the Mitton-McKellars
T.M.

With lots of love and thanks to the best family in the world
L.M.

First published 2000 by Walker Books Ltd
87 Vauxhall Walk, London SE11 5HJ

This edition published 2008

2 4 6 8 10 9 7 5 3 1

Text © 2000 Tony Mitton

Illustrations © 2000 Liz Million

This book has been typeset in Myriad Tilt Bold.

Printed in China

British Library Cataloguing in Publication Data:
a catalogue record for this book is available from the British Library.

ISBN 978-1-4063-1679-7

www.walkerbooks.co.uk